I0830774

THE KING OF WORTSER

The King of Wortser
Copyright © 2017 Jonathan Hermel
ISBN-13: 9780692917480
ISBN-10: 0692917489

All rights reserved. No part of this book may be reproduced or transmitted in any form or by any electronic or mechanical means, including photocopying, recording or by any information storage and retrieval system, without the written permission of the author.

THE KING OF WORTSER

by
Jonathan Hermel

Art by
Madalyn McLeod

He awoke from his slumber one bright afternoon.
The sun hung in the sky like a blazing balloon.
Then King Barney looked out to his kingdom below,
From the second floor window – *All's well! Good to go!*

He wagged his strong tail and his golden fur glistened
While cats chased the squirrels – those cats never listened
When Barney barked loudly, "Get off of my lawn!"
Well, that Blackjack meowed – still, it was kind of fun.

But the life of a king's not all glory and fame,
For protecting his subjects is part of the game.
Even Lola and Vinny, though violent and snide,
He defended like kin cross the Wortser Divide.

A good day to be lazy – or so Barney thought.
He yawned, stretched his tongue…oh, but then a new plot –
A glint from the sun struck his eye—there it was!
The white truck of the man he disliked—just because!

4

Just like *that* our King Barney was ready for battle
And ran down the stairs with a thunderous rattle.
The mailman walked up to the house, full of worry
As the king chose to greet him with barks full of fury.

He bounced through the office and out the backdoor,
To the gate on the side and barked loudly some more.
How dare he intrude! Barney showed him what-for!
Set a foot on my porch? A declaration of war!

The tall man smiled meekly and started away,
But I can't let him win – not again…not today!
Oh, but this was not done—a king's job never ceases.
Barney scratched at the gate till he tore it to pieces.

Barney dashed through the driveway and let out a roar…
Well, the man dropped his bag, then stood fused to the floor!
He ran for his truck with the king close behind,
Slammed the door, turned the key in a stressed state of mind.

Barns' was king of this block, so he ran down the street.
(Was there more to this world?) Oh, the freedom was sweet.
Now he chased the white truck, he was hot on his trail.
He followed him closely, but not for his mail!

The truck was much faster, but if he could catch it
He'd chew it to bits, use his claws like a hatchet,
Then he'd climb to the treetops and catch all the squirrels,
Take a car in his jaws – he was king of this world!

He ran like the wind as the truck sped away,
Getting further and further and further astray.
Barney rounded the corner then paused for a breather.
When he looked for the man or the truck, he saw neither!

Barney stopped and just stood there, accepting defeat.
He was there, all alone, in the midst of the street…
Then he peered all around at the houses that ringed him,
But all was so strange—he was out of his kingdom!

Oh my gosh! He was lost! What's our Barney to do?
He looked left; he looked right, but he hadn't a clue.
Then a honk and a screech and a great engine roaring!
Barney leapt to the curb—well, so much for exploring!

He was stirred but not shaken; the king longed for home,
With a family to pet him and his favorite bone.
Then two mean kids on bikes—they ran over his tail!
They just pointed and laughed at poor Barney's sad wail.

The birds and the squirrels even laughed at his pain
As a car splashed a puddle of yesterday's rain
On poor Barney. He lay there…the king felt so small.
This world wasn't friendly…not friendly at all!

So unlike his kingdom, these folks didn't care
If he was the king or some mean grizzly bear.
But he rose to his feet, then barked twice and stood tall.
He would find his way home – he's the king, after all!

Now every great journey begins with a step
But after his run he'd lost all of his pep.
Still, he walked down the road with each small step unknown,
Boldly hoping his path would lead back to his throne.

He was wandering this way and that down the road,
Beyond houses and trees and a lawn freshly mowed.
His tummy was growling…he smelled some fried chicken!
As he followed his nose his steps started to quicken…

He was licking his chops, and just *as* he was hopin'
He walked into a yard – hey, the gate…it was open.
He spied right before him a platter from heaven –
Steaming country-fried drumsticks – at least six or seven!

He scarfed them all down – it was just so delicious!
But he had to act fast – the man looked pretty vicious!
He ran toward the king with a long-handled shovel,
But Barney escaped now without any trouble.

He jumped a white fence and then zoomed down the street.
Oh, that's right! He's still lost! (Freedom wasn't so sweet!)
Barney *just* wanted home! Yes, his lesson was learned,
But the streets are too many! Which way should he turn?

Then his eye spotted something that might save the day!
A long trail of paw prints! Might this lead the way?
To his kingdom on Wortser with all of his friends!
Oh, maybe this nightmare will happily end!

Like a private detective he followed the trail
Of tiny-sized paw prints – right to a dog's tail!
The small furry beast was just out for a walk
With a sweet little lady who went into shock.

Barney shuddered and shook, now accepting his fate.
His king's life was over, the hour was late…
The long shadows around him were scary like ghosts,
Soon the lamps would be lighted on top of the posts.

So long, cruel world…it's been a nice ride.
Now the goblins will get me – there's nowhere to hide.
The sad dog curled up in a ball on the ground,
Now the great King of Wortser was nobody's hound.

He dreamt of his throne and the ones he so loved
And sent them dog kisses on wings of a dove.
He closed both his eyes…but then this old pup
Sprung up to his feet. *I don't ever give up!*

He took a deep breath, shook his head, and stood tall.
I won't ever give up! I'm the king, after all!
But what he saw next – was it good or bad luck?
Just then down the street came a little white truck.

Should he stay? Should he run? Daylight now was quite dim,
As the tall man got out of the truck – *it was him.*
"Hi, Barney," he said – oh, but this was his foe!
Barney froze in his tracks. Should he stay? Should he go?

Barney tried a weak growl as the mailman just smiled.
Should he bite? Not tonight – it's no time to go wild.
The man sat on his heels then rose up to his feet,
And he held out his hand – he was holding a treat!

Barney sniffed at the snack and then gobbled it down,
"Don't worry there, pup, you were lost, now you're found."
This man wasn't horrid – in fact he was nice!
Perhaps in the future, Barns' ought to think twice.

The man walked to the truck and then nodded his head.
"Let's get you back home to your castle," he said.
They drove down the street then turned left and turned right,
And before long his kingdom was clearly in sight!

It was good to be home to those sweet hugs and kisses!
Even Vinny's loud barks and old Blackjack's shrill hisses
Were so great to come home to, and not any hassle.
Once again mighty Barney was king of his castle!

What's the lesson, he wondered, now back at his post?
Maybe sometimes your rivals can help you the most!
He understood one thing – that he'd never roam
And risk losing his family, his kingdom, his home.

All the *best* things in life, *all* of them are right here –
Even those that we bark at are precious and dear.
Barney looked out the window, then closed his sore eyes
And dreamt he was king – but now humble and wise.

When the birds brought the sun – oh, the sky looked so blue!
Barney jumped to his feet and looked out to the view
Of his friends and his kingdom – hey! There's the white truck
And the man that had saved him from all his bad luck.

Barney barked very loudly (in friendship not fury!)
And ran to the boarded up gate in a hurry.
The man rubbed Barney's head and said, "Hello, my friend!"
It's a brand new beginning! This *is* not the end!

www.ingramcontent.com/pod-product-compliance
Lightning Source LLC
Chambersburg PA
CBHW041152300726
48981CB00003B/238